PUFFIN BOOKS

Whizziwig

Malorie Blackman is an ex computer-programmer who now writes full time. She has had a number of jobs, including database manager, systems programmer, receptionist and shop assistant. As a database manager she travelled extensively to places such as Toronto, Geneva, New York and Dallas.

Not So Stupid! her first collection of short stories was a Selected Twenty title for Feminist Book Fortnight, 1991. Since then she has published over fifteen books, including *Hacker*, which won both the W. H. Smith Mind-Boggling Books Award and the *Young Telegraph*/Gimme 5 Children's Book of the Year Award in 1994, and the *Girl Wonder* series. She has contributed to numerous anthologies for both adults and children. She lives in London with her partner and several pets, including a frog, some bears, an owl, a haggis, a whale and a penguin – all stuffed toys!

Rosie

Other books by Malorie Blackman

GIRL WONDER AND THE TERRIFIC TWINS
GIRL WONDER TO THE RESCUE

JACK SWEETTOOTH THE 73RD

Malorie Blackman

Whizziwig

Illustrated by Stephen Lee

PUFFIN BOOKS

To Neil, with love,
And to my darling Junior

PUFFIN BOOKS

Published by the Penguin Group
Penguin Books Ltd, 27 Wrights Lane, London W8 5TZ, England
Penguin Books USA Inc., 375 Hudson Street, New York, New York 10014, USA
Penguin Books Australia Ltd, Ringwood, Victoria, Australia
Penguin Books Canada Ltd, 10 Alcorn Avenue, Toronto, Ontario, Canada M4V 3B2
Penguin Books (NZ) Ltd, 182–190 Wairau Road, Auckland 10, New Zealand

Penguin Books Ltd, Registered Offices: Harmondsworth, Middlesex, England

First published by Viking 1995
Published in Puffin Books 1997
5 7 9 10 8 6

Text copyright © Oneta Malorie Blackman, 1995
Illustrations copyright © Stephen Lee, 1995
All rights reserved

The moral right of the author has been asserted

Filmset in Baskerville

Made and printed in England by Clays Ltd, St Ives plc

Contents

Chapter One

Nothing Scary

'Mum, Dad, can I sleep with the light on? Please. *Please*,' Ben begged.

Mum shook her head. 'Now, Ben, we've been through all this before. There's nothing scary in this room.'

'But there *is*. It's small and furry and it b-bounces about.' Ben tried to swallow down the lump stuck in his throat. 'A-And it only comes out after you've switched off the light.'

Ben watched as his mum and dad exchanged a glance, their eyebrows raised. They didn't believe him . . .

'It's true. Honest!' Ben pleaded.

Ben looked around his bedroom. It looked all right now. Perfectly normal. But Ben knew there was something ... He stood behind his mum and dad at his bedroom door. He didn't want to go any further into the room. The *something* might be in there – just waiting to leap out at him.

'Ben, there's nothing here,' Dad said gently. 'Look, I'll show you.'

Dad walked over to the bed, where he squatted down and lifted up the duvet which trailed down to the carpet. He peered into the dark shadows beneath the bed.

'See, Ben. Nothing under there.'

Ben winced as Dad stuck his arm under the bed and waved it about. Then Dad stood up and went over to the wardrobe.

'And there's nothing in here either.' Dad flung open the door.

Ben flinched, but then looked. His dad was right. The wardrobe was full of his clothes, but nothing else.

'There are no bad things anywhere in your room or this house for that matter,' said Mum. 'Nothing bad could get past us.'

'But –' Ben began.

'No buts, Ben!' Mum interrupted. 'You're just having bad dreams.'

'And you know why, don't you?' Dad frowned. 'This all started last Saturday when you sneaked behind the sofa to watch the late-night horror film.'

Mum nodded as she remembered. 'Yeah! We didn't catch you until the film was half over. That's where all this has come from.

Watching that film has given you nightmares.'

'Mum, it *wasn't* the horror film and I'm *not* having nightmares,' Ben said. 'There's something in this room and it waits till it's dark and then –'

'Ben, if you carry on like this, you'll never get any sleep.' Mum sighed. 'OK, we'll leave the light on – but only for tonight. Do you want Tarzan with you?'

Tarzan was their black-and-white dog with a slobbery tongue.

Ben shook his head. 'No thanks, Mum.'

To tell the truth, Ben was a bit frightened of Tarzan too. When Tarzan got excited, he would whirl about and leap up at people.

No, as long as the light was left on then Ben would be all right. That way the *something* couldn't leap out and bounce about and surprise him.

But he still had to get across his bedroom to his bed. Ben took a deep breath, then another. Then he sprinted across the room, his feet barely touching the carpet. He leapt into his bed, pulling the duvet up to his nose.

'Goodnight, Mum, goodnight, Dad,' Ben said.

Ben's mum and dad kissed him goodnight. They left the bedroom, shutting the door behind them but remembering to leave the light on. Ben could hear them talking although he couldn't make out the exact words. The sound faded as they walked downstairs.

I bet I know what they're talking about, Ben thought sadly. I wish I was more like

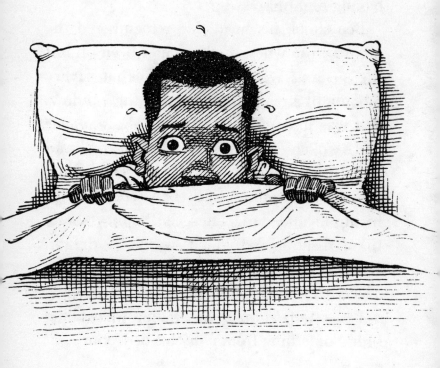

Splitter Lawson at school. He's not afraid of anything. I'm afraid of everything, even my own dog.

Ben felt totally miserable. If only he was brave and fearless – like Splitter. Then he would stand in the middle of his bedroom and demand that the bouncy something show itself.

Slowly, Ben looked around. The room was brightly lit and still. Maybe . . . maybe he *was* imagining things? Maybe he *was* just having nightmares . . .?

Ben shook his head. He remembered the night before when the light had been off but the curtains weren't drawn, so that silvery moonlight streamed in through the window. Ben was just nodding off when the *something* had woken him up by bouncing and bouncing and BOUNCING around the room – until Ben screamed for his mum and dad. Then the bouncy something disappeared. That wasn't a dream. Ben was sure it wasn't.

'Ben . . . Ben . . .'

Ben sat up at once. Something was calling him. Something from *inside* his bedroom . . .

Chapter Two

Whizziwig Appears

'Who . . . who's there?' Ben squeaked. 'My name is Whizziwig. I am sorry if I frightened you. I did not mean to. I would have spoken to you before, but it has taken me this long to learn all the spoken languages on this planet.'

Ben looked here, there and everywhere, but he could see nothing. Whatever it was, it spoke with a soft, low, echoey voice that made Ben's ears tingle. His heart hammered and he felt perspiration running down into the corner of one of his eyes, but he was too scared even to wipe it away.

'Where are you?' he whispered.

'On top of the wardrobe,' the voice answered. 'Can I come down now?'

Ben stared at the top of the wardrobe. All he could see was the suitcase used whenever he and Mum and Dad went on holiday or when they went to stay with Gran.

'Are you behind the suitcase?' Ben asked.

'That is correct. Can I come down now?' the voice asked again.

'Er . . . I suppose so,' Ben said slowly.

He wasn't too sure if he wanted the

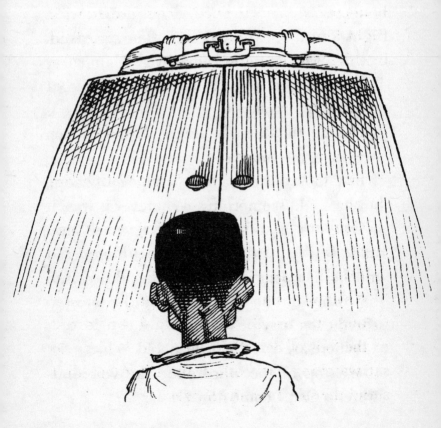

whatever-it-was to come down. But before he could change his mind, something that looked like a small globe covered with golden brown fur edged out from behind the suitcase. It had tiny arms like handles coming out of its sides, two silver-coloured eyes and a round, fur-covered mouth.

The strange something bounced down from the top of the wardrobe and started bouncing towards the bed. Ben squealed with fright and drew back against the wall, pulling his duvet with him.

Whizziwig froze in mid-air. 'What is wrong?'

'D-Do you have to bounce around l-like that?' Ben whispered.

'But that is how I move,' said Whizziwig, puzzled.

'Couldn't you move a bit slower then? Just until I get used to you,' Ben said.

'OK.'

Whizziwig moved slowly, oh so slowly, through the air before coming down to rest at the foot of Ben's bed. Ben and Whizziwig sat watching each other, until Ben couldn't stand the suspense any longer.

'What are you?' Ben asked.

'I am an Oricon,' Whizziwig said. 'What the people on your world would call a wish-giver.'

'Are you from outer space then?' Ben leaned forward eagerly. 'Are you from Mars?'

'Hardly,' Whizziwig sniffed. 'I am from a lot further away than that.'

Ben's eyes narrowed. 'So what're you doing in my bedroom then?'

This couldn't be one of Splitter Lawson's tricks – could it? Splitter Lawson was in Ben's class and he liked to show people up by playing stupid jokes.

'I was passing your planet four days ago on my way to visit my auntie, when some space debris hit my ship and I had to make an emergency landing on your roof,' said Whizziwig.

'Are you a boy or a girl?' asked Ben.

Whizziwig sounded a bit like a girl, but he couldn't be sure.

'We do not have boys and girls on Oricon in the same way that you do on Earth,' Whizziwig tried to explain. 'But if it helps you, I suppose I am closer to a girl as you would know it than anything else.'

'Oh, I see,' said Ben, not sure that he saw much at all. He sat back. 'Where's your ship now? Can I see it?'

'It is still up on your roof. It will have to stay there until I can fix it.' Whizziwig sighed. 'I have been bouncing around this immediate area ever since I arrived and I have yet to fix a single thing.'

'I'll . . . I'll help you fix your ship if you like,' Ben offered. He wasn't quite sure how he'd get up on the roof but he really wanted to see Whizziwig's spaceship.

'Are you a wish-giver too?' Whizziwig asked hopefully.

'No. Should I be?' asked Ben.

'I am afraid so,' said Whizziwig. 'It will take wishes to fix my ship.'

'I don't understand,' said Ben, not holding on quite so tightly to his duvet any more.

'As I said, I am a wish-giver,' said Whizziwig. 'And I can only fix my ship by giving people whatever they wish for.'

'So if I wish for a new bicycle, will you give me one?' Ben asked excitedly.

'It does not quite work like that —'
Whizziwig began.

'Oh, please can I have a new bike? I wish I had a mountain bike,' Ben pleaded. 'My bike is ancient and it's only got a measly three gears.'

Whizziwig rocked to the left and then to the right.

'Nope!' she said.

'But you said you were a wish-giver,' Ben argued.

'I can only grant wishes if you make a wish for someone else,' Whizziwig said.

'Oh!' Ben slumped back against the head-board. He thought long and hard.

'How about if I wish for a mountain bike for Dad but in my size?' Ben asked hopefully.

'Nope! It does not work that way either,' said Whizziwig. 'You have to wish almost without realizing what you're doing – it has to be unselfish wishing.'

'But that doesn't make sense. How can

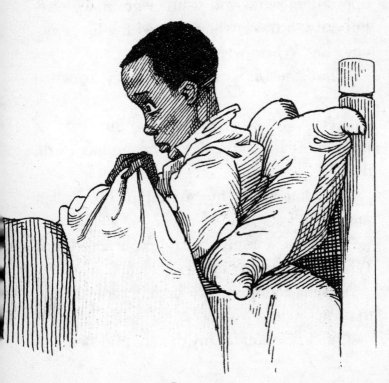

19.

you wish for something without realizing that you're wishing in the first place?' Ben frowned.

The Oricon put out her hands. 'That is the way it works. I am an accidental wish-giver.'

'I don't get it,' said Ben.

'There are different types of Oricons. Some make dreams come true, others make day-dreams come true, some give you exactly what you want, some give you the exact opposite of what you want. I grant wishes – but only to those who make wishes for some-one else,' Whizziwig explained.

'That's a bit strange, isn't it?' frowned Ben.

'Very!' Whizziwig agreed. 'But that is my job. It is tough, but someone has to do it!'

'So what about my mountain bike?' Ben said.

'I cannot comply. Sorry! You see –' But Whizziwig got no further.

At that moment, the door handle began to turn.

'Quick. Get under my duvet,' said Ben.

With one bounce, Whizziwig was at the top of the bed. She slid under the duvet just as the bedroom door was opened.

Mum came in and before anyone could stop him, Tarzan the dog bounded into the room and raced straight for the bed.

Chapter Three

Down, Tarzan!

'Mum! MUM! Stop him!' Ben called out. Tarzan's front paws were up on the bed and he barked madly, his tail wagging like a flag in a hurricane. Ben knew that Tarzan wasn't barking at him. Tarzan had smelt or sensed that Whizziwig was under the duvet and was trying to get to her.

Ben put himself between Whizziwig and Tarzan. Frantically, he tried to push Tarzan down as the dog leapt up on to the bed.

'MUM!' Ben shouted.

'Tarzan! Down, Tarzan! Bad dog!' Mum came over and took hold of Tarzan's collar, dragging him off the bed.

Tarzan carried on barking at the top of his voice.

'Tarzan! Behave yourself!' Mum said sternly. 'And you should know better than to jump up on the bed!'

Mum had to drag Tarzan out of the room. The dog obviously didn't want to leave – his gaze never once left Ben's bed. Mum put Tarzan out into the hall, shutting the door firmly behind him.

'What has got into that dog?' Mum muttered. 'Are you all right, Ben?'

Ben nodded and asked, 'What's the matter, Mum? Why did you come into my room?'

'I was outside the door and I thought I heard voices,' Mum frowned.

'I . . . I was just talking to myself,' Ben replied.

'Hhmm! Well, fascinating as the conversation might be, I think you should leave the rest for tomorrow morning. It's time you were asleep,' smiled Mum.

'OK,' Ben said. 'Goodnight, Mum.'

'Goodnight, Ben.' Mum left the room, shutting the door behind her.

Whizziwig rose upwards to hover about thirty centimetres off the bed.

'I can see that Tarzan creature and I are

not going to be best friends,' Whizziwig
sniffed.

Ben sighed with relief. 'I was worried there
for a minute. I thought Tarzan would get
you for sure.'

'Not if I have anything to do with it!'
Whizziwig scoffed. 'Now, if you don't mind,
I think I'll shut down for a while. It's been a
very busy day and that Tarzan creature has
drained the last of my primary energy.'

'Shut down?' Ben asked.

'I think you humans call it sleep,' said
Whizziwig.

'Oh, all right,' Ben said, disappointed. 'I

was hoping you'd tell me about your planet – what's it called? Oricon? And about some of the wishes you've granted. And all about –'

'Some other time,' Whizziwig said. 'If I don't shut down now, I won't be in a fit state to fix my ship.'

Whizziwig started to bounce towards the wardrobe.

'I hope you don't mind if I sleep here again tonight?' she asked. And with one bounce Whizziwig was on top of the suitcase, on top of the wardrobe.

'But it might not be safe,' Ben said, worried. 'Mum or Dad might find you. Tarzan might bark up at you until Mum takes down the suitcase to see what he's barking at.'

'Oh! Where should I sleep then?' Whizziwig asked.

Ben looked around his room. What would be a good hiding place? The chest of drawers? No, they wouldn't do. Mum was always putting things in them. Inside the wardrobe? No. The same problem. Behind the chair? No, Tarzan might get Whizziwig then.

'I know!' Ben bounced up and down on his bed. 'You can sleep under my bed. No one will look for you there and Tarzan can't get under there – he's too big.'

'Hhmm! Are you sure?'

'Positive,' Ben smiled.

Whizziwig bounced once, bounced twice, then bounced on to the floor, before rolling under the edge of the duvet and out of sight. Ben flung the duvet aside and turned upside-down to stick his head under the bed. It was shadowy and he could only just see Whizziwig in the corner by the wall.

'Goodnight, Whizziwig,' Ben said.

'Goodnight, Ben,' said Whizziwig.

Ben straightened up to lie flat, his hands folded behind his head. Should he sneak out of the room and tell Mum and Dad about Whizziwig? Ben finally decided against it. From the films he'd seen on television, sometimes grown-ups acted very strangely when they met aliens from other planets.

But I was right. I *knew* there was something in my room, Ben grinned to himself. I just knew it!

Suddenly he had a thought.

There was one wish, one special wish that Ben wanted more than anything else in the world – even more than the mountain bike.

'Whizziwig, if I wish a special wish, will you make it come true? It's not for me – not really. And it's really important. If you make this one wish come true, I promise I won't wish for anything else ever again and I'll help you mend your spaceship.'

Ben stuck his head beneath the bed again. Very softly, very carefully, he made his wish. Silence.

'Whizziwig? Are you awake . . . ?' Ben whispered.

But there was no reply.

Chapter Four

Flapping at Both Ends

When Ben woke up the next morning, the sun was shining, he could hear birds singing and it was Sunday – the best day of the week! Ben lay still for a moment, trying to remember something important.

'Ben, come downstairs for your breakfast,' Mum called out.

Ben sniffed the air. Bacon and toast! Brill!

'Coming, Mum,' he called back.

He threw back his duvet and leapt out of bed. Unfortunately, Whizziwig had chosen just that moment to roll out from beneath the bed. Ben stepped on Whizziwig and went flying backwards. Luckily he landed on his duvet.

'I would appreciate it if you did *not* step

on my head first thing in the morning,'
Whizziwig declared. She rose up to hover
just above Ben.

'Sorry, Whizziwig!' Ben grinned. 'I must
admit, I almost thought I'd dreamt you.
How are you?'

'My primary energy has returned, thank
you,' Whizziwig replied. 'And how are you?'

'Hungry! I'm going down for my breakfast,' Ben said. 'Why don't you check your
ship or something until I get back?'

'Nope, I think I will watch you eat,'
Whizziwig decided. 'Before I came to your
planet I had never seen creatures eating. It
is most interesting.'

'Don't you eat then?' Ben asked,
surprised.

'Not like humans,' said Whizziwig. 'I live
on wishes.'

'Oh, I scc,' said Ben. He couldn't imagine
not having to eat. He would miss chips and
bacon and ice-cream too much. 'Well, if you
do come downstairs just make sure that
Mum and Dad don't see you,' Ben added.

'They have not seen me yet, have they?'
Whizziwig winked.

'Tarzan has. You'd better keep out of his way,' Ben warned.

'Do not worry! Wherever Tarzan goes, I will *not* follow!'

Ben ran downstairs with Whizziwig bouncing down behind him. Just as he reached the hall, the doorbell rang. Whizziwig bounced up above the door and floated just below the ceiling.

'You can't stay there,' Ben hissed frantically. 'Someone will see you.'

'They will not. No one is going to look up
here,' Whizziwig replied.

Ben wanted to argue, but the doorbell
rang again. After a nervous glance directed
at Whizziwig, Ben opened the door.

'Hello, Ben. Are your mum and dad in?'

Ben groaned. It was Mrs Florence Leonard
from next door. Mum and Dad called her
Flapping Florence when they thought Ben
wasn't around to hear them. Mrs Leonard
was the most gossipy busybody in the world.
And she was always spreading rumours.

'Ben, who is it?' Dad came out of the
kitchen. 'Oh . . .' he said faintly. 'Oh, hello,
Mrs Leonard.'

Dad didn't look too pleased to see their
neighbour either.

'Hello, Mr Sinclair.' Mrs Leonard pushed
Ben aside and walked into the house. 'Is
that bacon I smell?' She pushed past Dad
and walked into the kitchen. Ben looked
at Dad and Dad looked at Ben and they
both wrinkled up their noses.

'Hello, Mrs Sinclair,' Mrs Leonard said to

Mum. 'I really shouldn't, but some bacon and toast would be most welcome.'

'Hello, Mrs Leonard. Have a seat.' Mum tried to smile.

'And I'll have a nice cup of tea as well, if you're asking,' said Mrs Leonard, plonking herself down at the kitchen table.

'Did you hear anyone ask, Ben? 'Cause I didn't!' Dad muttered. Ben's mum gave him a warning look.

Ben glanced up. Whizziwig was outside the kitchen, still floating just below the ceiling. Ben was sure his heart would burst through his chest at any second. What if someone should see Whizziwig? What would happen then?

'I can't stay too long,' Mrs Leonard said.

'Thank goodness for that,' Dad mumbled.

Mum gave Dad another look. Mum had good ears, even if Mrs Leonard didn't. Mrs Leonard pulled a plate of bacon and beans on toast towards her.

'Delicious!' she said, tucking in.

Ben watched with dismay as what looked suspiciously like his breakfast disappeared down his next-door neighbour's throat.

'I just popped round for a chat.' Mrs Leonard dusted some toast crumbs off the table in front of her. 'How are all of you?'

But before anyone could even open their mouths to reply, Mrs Leonard started!

'Have you heard? Mr Johnson from number fifty-two has got a new car again. That must be the third new car this year and summer has barely started yet! Where does he get the money from? That's what I'd like to know.' Mrs Leonard was well away now. 'And Mrs Vester has bought her Sarah a new tricycle. If you ask me she spoils that daughter of hers . . .'

'Ben, come on,' Mum said. 'I'll take you upstairs for your shower.'

Mum pushed Ben out of the kitchen. Dad tried to follow. 'No, you stay here and keep Mrs Leonard company.' Mum smiled sweetly.

Dad didn't look best pleased – to say the least! Mum followed Ben up the stairs.

'All that woman does is gossip, gossip. She doesn't even pause to draw breath,' Mum muttered. 'She talks so much her tongue must be hinged in the middle so it can flap at both ends! That way if one end gets tired, the other end can take over!'

'Mum, what about my breakfast?' Ben said, dismayed. He didn't care about hinged and flapping tongues. But he did care about his breakfast!

'I'll make you some more after you've had your shower,' Mum said.

Ben could see that Mum was still fuming about their neighbour. Ben decided to ask

Dad to cook his breakfast. In her current mood, Mum would only burn it!

'D'you know, I wish that woman's tongue *was* hinged in the middle,' said Mum. 'And I wish that when she started gossiping, one half of her tongue would tell her off every time the other half of her tongue got started!'

And that's when the trouble began.

Chapter Five

It's Not Me!

Ben and Mum reached the top of the stairs. Ben looked around for Whizziwig but she was nowhere in sight. Ben was worried. He couldn't help it, even though he had a sort of Christmas *and* birthday feeling swirling around in his stomach. Something good-tremendous or bad-tremendous was about to happen. But what?

All of a sudden there was a terrible shriek.

'AAARRRRGGHH!'

They both froze.

'What on earth . . .? That's Mrs Leonard,' Mum said.

Mum raced down the stairs and into the kitchen, closely followed by Ben. Mrs Leonard was on her feet, staring at Dad.

'Don't do that, Mr Sinclair! It's very cruel of you . . .' Mrs Leonard screamed.

'Not as cruel as you've been over the years – spreading rumours and gossip and hurting people's feelings!'

Ben stared at Mrs Leonard. He could hardly believe it and he certainly didn't understand it, but that last remark had definitely come from Mrs Leonard's mouth.

'Daniel, what are you doing?' Mum frowned at Dad.

'I'm not doing anything,' Dad protested. 'Mrs Leonard has gone off her head and right round the twist. She's talking to herself.'

'I'm not talking to myself,' Mrs Leonard squealed.

'Yes, you are! Besides, who else would want to talk to you?' Mrs Leonard's mouth opened, but her words were as much of a surprise to her as they were to everyone else in the kitchen. More so, to judge by the look on her face. Her hands flew to her throat, her lips were pressed tight together until they were just one thin line and her eyes were as big as dinner plates. Her gaze darted around the room as if she still couldn't believe that the words were coming from her mouth.

'Mum, what's the matter with Mrs Leonard?' Ben frowned.

'I don't know,' Mum said slowly.

'There's nothing wrong with me,' Mrs Leonard quaked.

'Nothing that a good padlock on your mouth couldn't cure.' Mrs Leonard had opened her mouth and the words just fell out.

'Daniel, are you sure . . .?' Mum began.

'I promise, it's not me!' Dad denied.

'I'm asleep – that's what it is! I'm dreaming!' said Mrs Leonard, nodding her head vigorously. 'I'll wake up in a minute.'

'It's a pity your tongue never goes to

sleep . . .' Once again, the words just spilled out of Mrs Leonard's mouth.

'AAARRRGGGGGGHHHHHH!' Mrs Leonard clapped both hands over her mouth and ran screaming from the kitchen. Moments later the front door was slammed shut.

Ben, Mum and Dad stared at each other. Then they burst out laughing! Until soon all three of them were holding their stomachs, tears of laughter running down their cheeks.

'Well! I know I said that woman should have her tongue hinged in the middle but this is ridiculous!' Mum wiped the tears from her eyes.

Immediately Ben stopped laughing. Whizziwig! Ben looked around. There, just visible above the front door was the Oricon. Ben ran out of the kitchen.

'Whizziwig, was that you?' Ben whispered. 'Did you make Mum's wish about Mrs Leonard's tongue come true?'

Whizziwig grinned. 'Yup! And she made two wishes actually. So that is my spon-bungulator and my parflange fixed! Two items down, only twenty-one to go!'

'What d'you mean – only twenty-one to go?' said Ben, worried.

'Twenty-three items on my ship were in need of repair, therefore I have to grant twenty-three wishes. With your mother's two wishes that leaves me only twenty-one more wishes to grant before my ship is completely repaired and ready to leave this planet,' said Whizziwig. 'At last I feel I am getting somewhere! I have actually started to repair my ship.'

'But you can't go round granting wishes to people who don't mean them,' Ben said quickly. 'People wish for all kinds of things they don't really mean. And what about Mrs Leonard's tongue? How's she going to talk to anyone with her tongue hinged in the middle and arguing with her all the time?'

Whizziwig frowned. 'I thought that was the whole point.'

'Whizziwig!'

'Do not worry! My wishes only last for ninety thousand and sixty-one yenvings – except in very special circumstances!' smiled Whizziwig.

'*How long* . . .?' Ben squeaked.

Even Mrs Leonard didn't deserve to have her tongue quarrel with her for the rest of her life and beyond. And poor Mrs Leonard didn't have much time left anyway. She was ancient. Thirty-five, at least!

'Ninety thousand and sixty-one yenvings add up to one whole day and night, one hour, one minute and one second on your planet,' said Whizziwig. 'A little after this time tomorrow morning, your neighbour will be back to her usual self.'

Ben sighed with relief. 'Thank goodness for that!

'I think I will go and check on my spon-bungulator and my parflange,' Whizziwig said. 'Is your window open? Can I still get to the roof that way?'

Ben nodded.

'See you tonight then,' said Whizziwig.

'Tonight? Won't I see you before then?' asked Ben, dismayed.

'Nope, it will take all day to reset my sponbungulator and check the star chart information in my parflange. But I will be with you before you go to sleep,' said Whizziwig.

'But I wanted to ask you all sorts of questions,' said Ben. 'And I have to go to bed early tonight. I've got to go to school tomorrow.'

'School – a place of learning and knowledge!' Whizziwig said eagerly. 'I have questions to ask about this place. I shall come with you tomorrow and learn about your school.'

'Oh, but . . . but . . .'

'See you later, Ben,' said Whizziwig.

And before Ben could say another word, Whizziwig tucked in her arms and off she went, bouncing against the ceiling as she made her way upstairs.

'Ben, who are you talking to?' Dad popped his head out from the kitchen to ask.

'Er . . . just myself, Dad. Just myself.' Ben gave a weak smile.

Dad frowned. 'First sign of madness, you know. You don't want to end up like Mrs Leonard, do you?'

Ben shook his head vigorously. No, he most certainly did not!

'Come for your breakfast, Ben,' called Mum.

Slowly, Ben walked into the kitchen. Already he could see that having Whizziwig around, granting wishes left, right and centre, was going to be tricky. In fact, worse than tricky . . . trouble! But it was also going to be FUN!

Chapter Six

The Kissing Wish

The next morning after breakfast, Ben sneaked Whizziwig into his school back-pack.

'Whizziwig, don't say a word until we leave the house,' whispered Ben.

Ben pulled on his jacket and flung his back-pack over his shoulder.

'Ouch! Careful!' Whizziwig exclaimed as she bounced off Ben's back.

'Shush!' Ben pleaded. Then in a louder voice he said, 'I'm off now, Mum. See you later.'

Mum's head appeared over the upstairs banister. 'OK, Ben. See you –' She didn't get any further.

Without warning, Tarzan came rushing

out of the living-room, barking madly. He rushed at Ben, jumping up at his back-pack.

'Down, Tarzan. DOWN!' Ben said fiercely, holding up his back-pack over his head. 'I said, DOWN!' Ben spoke more firmly to Tarzan than he had ever done before.

And immediately Tarzan lay down. It was hard to say who was more surprised, Ben or the dog.

'And stay there!' said Ben, still annoyed.

'Well done, Ben,' said his mum.

Ben grinned up at her. He moved to the front door. Tarzan began to stand.

'Stay!' commanded Ben.

Tarzan lay down again.

'I do not like that dog – at all!' sniffed Whizziwig from inside the back-pack.

'Whizziwig, listen,' said Ben as they headed down the garden path. 'You've got to stay in my bag and not move. OK?'

'But I want to see your school and your friends and your teachers and –'

'Please, Whizziwig,' Ben pleaded. 'If someone sees you it could cause all kinds of problems.'

'Oh, if you insist,' Whizziwig agreed reluctantly. 'But I still have a lot of questions about your school.'

'But that's all we talked about last night,' Ben protested. 'When are you going to tell me about your planet Oricon?'

'Later! Later! Right now, I am more interested in learning about your school,' said Whizziwig.

And that's when Monday's trouble started!

Ben was in his classroom. The buzzer had sounded and everyone was waiting for Mr Archer, the teacher, to appear from the staff-room. Ben sat on a desk with some of his friends as his best friend Steven came over to him.

'Ben,' Steven began, his eyes twinkling. 'Guess what? Charlotte likes you.'

Ben felt his face begin to burn.

'Don't talk soft,' he sniffed.

'She does,' Steven insisted, with a laugh.

By now Ben's face was burning like a raging forest-fire.

'Charlotte's an idiot and I don't like her,' Ben fumed.

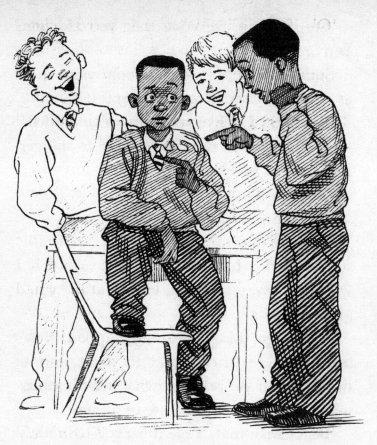

That wasn't strictly true. Ben did like
Charlotte, he just didn't want Charlotte
going around telling people that she liked
him. Ben glared at Steven, who was still
laughing at him. He looked around. All his
friends were laughing at him.

Ben marched straight up to Charlotte who
was chatting with some of her friends.

'Stop telling everyone that you like me,' Ben ordered.

Suddenly the whole classroom went quiet as everyone came closer to listen.

'But, Ben, I *do* like you,' Charlotte smiled.

All the boys in the class started to snigger. Ben's whole body was on fire now.

'No, you don't,' Ben argued.

'Yes, I do,' Charlotte replied.

'No, you don't.'

'Yes, I do. In fact I like you so much I wish that every time you looked at me you'd give me a kiss.'

A strange thing began to happen. Ben's lips began to prickle and to tickle and to tingle. Then he realized what was happening. Ben stared at Charlotte in dismay.

'Don't wish that. Take it back. *Take it back*,' Ben pleaded.

'I will not,' Charlotte said, her hands on her hips. 'I mean every word.'

Something like invisible hands pushed Ben forward. He tried his best to fight against it. He tried to stop his feet from moving forward a step at a time. He tried to stop his legs from working. But it was no good. With each tortured step, Ben got closer and closer to Charlotte. And the closer he got, the more his lips tingled.

'Whizziwig, no! Stop!' Ben called out, desperately.

Charlotte frowned at her friends. 'Who's Whizziwig?' she asked them. Her friends shrugged.

'Ben, what on earth are you doing?' Steven asked.

Ben was at Charlotte's side now. He couldn't answer. His lips had been taken over! To Ben's deep, DEEP embarrassment, he kissed Charlotte on the cheek.

Ben could hear his friends making puking noises or calling his name in stunned amazement. All Ben wanted to do was sink into the ground and disappear for ever.

'Ben, you traitor! You soppy, sissy traitor!' said Steven with disgust.

Charlotte turned to her giggling friends and said smugly, 'I *told* you he liked me.'

Ben stared at Charlotte in dismay. How could Whizziwig do this to him? How could she? Ben thought he couldn't be any more embarrassed than he already was, but he was wrong. Worse was to come.

Ben's lips had stopped tingling when he kissed Charlotte, but now that horrible tickling, prickling feeling was back. Before Ben

could stop himself, he kissed Charlotte again – and again, and *again*.

'Ben, I think that's enough now,' Charlotte frowned. 'You're showing me up!'

But Ben couldn't stop.

'Ben, that's enough!' Charlotte said annoyed.

Now her friends and Ben's friends were laughing at her.

'BEN SINCLAIR! UP HERE! NOW!' Mr Archer's angry voice had Ben's head snapping around. Everyone else scampered back to their seats.

The moment Ben turned his head to face his irate teacher, the weird sensation in his lips vanished – so at least that was something. But feeling more miserable than ever before in his life, Ben walked over to Mr Archer.

'Ben Sinclair, you are at school to exercise your brain, not your lips,' said Mr Archer. 'Sit at the front of the class for the rest of the day where I can keep an eye on you. Thea, swap places with Ben.'

Ben walked slowly over to his table to get his things. His head was bowed, his eyes focused on his feet and nothing else.

I'll never be able to face anyone ever again, Ben thought unhappily. He picked up his bag and felt Whizziwig wiggle inside it.

'I'll never forgive you for this – never, *ever*,' Ben muttered to Whizziwig.

'Your friend wished it for you,' Whizziwig whispered back. 'Do not blame me.'

Ben glanced up to make sure that no one had spotted him having a conversation with his bag. Big mistake!

Ben caught sight of Charlotte scowling at him. Immediately his lips began to quiver. No way was Ben going to kiss Charlotte again! Ben closed his eyes tight. The quivery, shivery tingle in his lips disappeared.

That was it! Charlotte wished that he'd kiss her every time he looked at her. So all Ben had to do for the next day and a bit was to make sure that he didn't look at Charlotte. Once he left school, he'd be fine. He just had to make sure that he didn't look at Charlotte before then.

'Ben, whenever you're ready,' Mr Archer drawled. 'And today I want you to sit outside the staff-room in the break-times, where I can keep an eye on you. You can eat your lunch outside the staff-room. Is that clear?'

Ben beamed at his teacher. 'Terrific! Yes, sir!'

Mr Archer frowned at Ben. 'As you're so happy about it, you can sit outside the staff-room for the rest of the week as well.'

Ben's heart sank. The rest of the week . . . He walked over to his new table. He'd only been at school for five minutes and already he was in more trouble than he'd ever been in, in his life. He'd kissed Charlotte, he was in trouble with his teacher and Charlotte had gone off him. He'd never be able to live it down. His friends would never let him hear the end of it. What a day! And it wasn't even lunch-time yet!

Chapter Seven

Bicycles

'**A**re you still not talking to me?' Whizziwig asked.

Ben clamped his lips even more firmly together. He was on his way home after the worst day of his life.

'Ben, it was not my fault,' Whizziwig said. 'The wish Charlotte made was for you, not for herself, so I had to grant it.'

'Hhmm!' Ben sniffed.

'Perhaps you would prefer it if I did not see you any more?' Whizziwig suggested.

'No!' Ben replied instantly. 'I mean . . . er . . . no, I suppose not.'

'Then cheer up,' smiled Whizziwig. 'No harm was done.'

'No harm?' Ben squeaked. 'The only

reason I'm talking to you at all is because Splitter Lawson wasn't at school today. I hate to think what would've happened if he *had* been at school. Whizziwig, the least you can do now is grant me my wish.'

'I have already told you, I cannot do that,' Whizziwig reminded him. 'You will just have to ask your mum and dad to buy you a bicycle —'

'I don't care about the bike. I wish Dad had a mountain bike. I wish Dad had a whole garden full of mountain bikes — all in his size! See! I don't care about the stupid mountain bike. What I really want, what I really wish for is . . . is a brother. I'd even settle for a sister.'

'I am not —' Whizziwig began.

But she didn't get much further.

'Ben! BEN!'

Ben turned around as Whizziwig ducked back down into his back-pack. It was Ben's best friend Steven calling him. Instantly Ben felt his face begin to burn with shame. Steven ran up to him, a huge grin on his face.

'Hi, Ben! You really had us fooled for a while.'

Ben frowned. 'What're you talking about?'

'We thought you really did like Charlotte until you showed her up. It was great,' smiled Steven.

Ben's whole body went burning hot, then burning cold.

'I didn't mean to show her up,' he muttered.

'Of course you did. You didn't really mean to kiss her, did you?' Steven frowned.

Ben didn't answer. They carried on walking.

'She really hates you now,' grinned Steven. 'Nice one!'

'Steven, I . . .'

'Yeah?'

'Never mind,' Ben sighed, giving up.

'Can I come round your house for a game of Super Mario?' Steven asked.

Ben nodded, his mind too full of other things to speak. What next? he wondered, what next?

He didn't have to wait long before his question was answered.

They turned the corner into Ben's road

and saw a large crowd gathered around Ben's house.

'What's going on?' Ben frowned, that uneasy, queasy feeling back in his stomach.

Ben and Steven looked at each other. Without either of them saying a word they both started running towards Ben's house.

'Excuse me. 'Scuse us please!' Ben and Steve pushed their way through the crowd.

And then they saw them! In Ben's front garden. Bicycles! Lying on their sides, standing upright, leaning against the front door –

they were everywhere. Piles and pillars of them. Masses and mounds of them. Heaps and hills of them. Filling the front garden and spilling out of the gate.

And from inside the house, Ben's mum yelled, 'Help! Call the police, someone! I can't get out of the front door!'

'Where did all these come from?' Steven asked breathlessly.

Ben didn't need to ask. He knew. Whizziwig!

'Steven, stay here,' Ben ordered, fighting his way to the back of the crowd.

'Whizziwig!' Ben opened up his bag. 'Did you do this?'

'Yup. You wished for a garden full of mountain bikes for your dad. And that is what you got,' said Whizziwig. 'Is there a problem?'

'But I didn't mean it,' squeaked Ben.

'You Earthlings never say what you mean or mean what you say,' said Whizziwig. 'Which is just as well, or I would never fix my ship and get home.'

'Whizziwig, do something. Please!' begged Ben. 'Mum can't get out of the house.'

'I cannot do anything. You wished for the bicycles,' said Whizziwig.

'Then I'll just unwish them!' said Ben, crossly. 'I wish all the bikes in our front garden were gone.'

Ben pushed back through the crowd again to see if it had worked. It hadn't.

'Whizziwig, why didn't you do it?' Ben whispered.

'You wished for something for yourself. I cannot grant those kind of wishes – remember?'

Just then, they heard Ben's mum again. 'Oh, I wish the police would come!'

Suddenly the wail of sirens filled the air, getting closer and closer. A fire engine and two police cars whizzed around the corner.

'Wow! This is better than any video game,' said Steven.

'Stand back. Everyone stand back,' said a policewoman, ushering the crowd away from Ben's front gate. 'That includes you, son,' she said to Ben.

'I live here. My mum's trapped in there,' Ben explained.

'Oh, I see. D'you know where all these bikes

have come from?' asked the policewoman.

Ben crossed his fingers behind his back. 'No idea,' he muttered.

'Don't worry. We'll soon have your mum out,' said a fireman who had joined them.

The firemen started lifting the bikes out of the garden and lining them up in the street.

Ben overheard two policemen talking.

'I've just checked. There've been no reports of any bikes stolen – not like these ones and certainly not as many,' said one policeman to the other.

'So where did they come from then?' asked the second policeman.

Ben didn't wait to hear any more. He watched as the mountain of bikes was slowly cleared out of the front garden. Ben glanced at the grown-ups around him. They all seemed to be enjoying what was going on.

Ben caught sight of Mrs Leonard, his next-door neighbour.

'Hello, Mrs Leonard,' he said faintly. He crossed his fingers, hoping against hope that she wouldn't want to gossip to him.

'Er . . . hello, Ben,' Mrs Leonard whispered. 'Where did all those bikes . . .?'

Mrs Leonard didn't finish her obvious question. She clamped her hand over her mouth.

'Are you all right, Mrs Leonard?' Ben asked, worried. Surely Whizziwig's wish must have worn off by now?

'I'm fine, thank you.' Mrs Leonard spoke quickly, clamping her lips together the moment the words were out.

Then Ben realized what Mrs Leonard was doing. The wish *had* worn off but Mrs Leonard couldn't know that. She was terrified she would start arguing with herself in front of all her neighbours. Ben wondered if he should try to explain, but he decided against it. She was a grown-up – and even if she did listen, she'd never believe him. She'd think he was just making fun of her.

Ben turned back to his house. His mum was still trapped in there.

'Whizziwig, do something.' Ben nudged his school-bag.

'I think I will shut down for a while,' said Whizziwig. 'Placing all those mountain bikes in your front garden has drained all my primary energy.'

'That's not the something I had in mind,' Ben argued.

No answer.

'Whizziwig? *Whizziwig!*' Ben hissed.

'Ben, why are you talking to your school-bag?' Steven asked curiously.

'Er, I wasn't. I was . . . er . . . just wondering how long it'll be before Mum can come out of the house.'

'Don't worry, Ben. Your mum will be fine,' Steven smiled.

Ben nodded.

And Steven was right. At last his mum emerged from the house, looking confused as well as very annoyed.

'Where on earth did all those bikes come from?' she asked.

They didn't come from anywhere on Earth, Ben thought. They came from a creature from Oricon – who was now fast asleep in Ben's school-bag.

Later that night as Ben and his mum and dad sat at the table having their dinner, Ben's dad said, 'I'd still like to know where all those bikes came from.'

'Hhmm!' said Ben's mum. 'It's obviously someone's feeble idea of a joke.'

'I hope we find out who, and soon,' said Ben's dad. 'If those bikes aren't claimed, the police said that all fifty bikes will belong to me. What do I want with fifty bikes? I don't even want one.'

'Ben, it's a shame they were all too big for you,' said Ben's mum. 'Then maybe you would've stopped pestering us about getting you a mountain bike.'

'Don't worry, Mum. I don't care if I never see another bike again for as long as I live,' Ben said. Then, thinking about it, he added, 'Well, I don't want to see another bike for the next couple of weeks anyway.'

With Whizziwig around, Ben wanted to make sure that he said what he meant and he meant what he said — even if he wasn't wishing. Who knew what might happen otherwise!

Chapter Eight

Splitter Lawson

The next day when Ben reached school, he immediately hid in the boys' toilets.

'Why are you hiding in here?' asked Whizziwig.

'You said the effect of your wishes lasts ninety thousand and something odd yenvings. Well, I've worked it out. I've still got to wait an hour, a minute and a second before Charlotte's wish wears off,' Ben explained. 'And I'm safer in here until the buzzer goes than in the playground, where I might see her accidentally.'

Whizziwig opened her mouth to speak but Ben interrupted her.

'And I know I'm a coward, so you don't need to tell me so.'

'I had no intention of saying any such thing,' said Whizziwig. 'And where did you get such a strange idea?'

Ben sighed. 'It's true. I am a coward. Everyone knows it. That's why I thought that if I had a younger brother, or even a sister, then that would be someone who doesn't know what a wimp I am. I would look after them and protect them and make sure that no one ever bullied them.'

'Ben, you are not a wimp.' Whizziwig frowned. 'Look at the way you saved me from your vicious dog, Tarzan – not once but twice.'

'I did do that, didn't I . . .' Ben smiled as he remembered. Then his smile faded. 'But I was still scared. I'm scared of my own dog.'

'It's even braver of you to stand up to Tarzan if you are afraid of him,' said Whizziwig. 'Being brave means overcoming your fears, acting in spite of being afraid.'

'Hhmm!' said Ben, thinking. 'I must admit, the funny thing is that now I've stood up to Tarzan, I'm not quite so scared of him any more.'

'I am!' said Whizziwig. 'Until my ship is

fixed, I intend to keep out of Tarzan's way completely.'

Just at that moment, the buzzer sounded. Ben left it until the very last moment before walking into his class, his head bent. Now if he could just make it to his table . . .

No such luck!

A pair of huge trainers, like two massive white-and-blue bricks, blocked his way.

Ben's heart bounced in his chest. He knew who those trainers belonged to – Splitter Lawson. He was called Splitter Lawson instead of Brian Lawson (which was his real name) because of the number of knees and lips he had split by pushing people over in the playground and punching people just for laughs. And while everyone in the class knew what Splitter was really like, it seemed the teachers had no idea. They thought Splitter was wonderful because he was always the one who offered to take messages around the school and carry the teachers' books. What they didn't know was that Splitter only did that to skive off his lessons and to bully anyone smaller than him that he might find in the corridors.

Ben glanced up at Splitter in dismay.

'I heard what you did yesterday,' Splitter grinned. 'And I'm –'

Mr Archer walked into the classroom.

'Is there a problem, Brian?' the teacher asked.

'No, Mr Archer,' Splitter replied.

'Then sit down,' said Mr Archer. 'Ben, I'm glad to see that you've decided to give your lips a rest for today, or were you contemplating kissing Brian?'

Ben sat down, his face on fire. He dropped his bag down on the floor from a greater height than was absolutely necessary.

'Ooof!' Whizziwig groaned, from inside the bag.

Ben concentrated on his work-books and the blackboard until the buzzer sounded for the mid-morning break.

'Sir, do I still have to sit outside the staff-room?' Ben asked.

From the look on Mr Archer's face, it was obvious that he'd completely forgotten about Ben's punishment.

'That depends,' frowned Mr Archer. 'D'you think you can keep your lips under control from now on?'

'Yes, sir. Don't worry! I promise I'm never going to kiss another girl for as long as I live,' Ben said earnestly.

Mr Archer's lips twitched. 'I somehow think that's one promise you won't be able to keep,' said the teacher. 'All right, Ben, you can go out and play, but behave yourself.'

And with that Mr Archer dashed off to

the staff-room, desperate for a cup of coffee and his pipe. At least half the class scurried out right behind him. Ben risked a quick glance at Charlotte.

Nothing! Not a tingle! Not a tickle! Not a prickle!

'Whizziwig! The wish has worn off,' Ben whispered excitedly.

'I am so glad,' sniffed Whizziwig.

'Oh well, I might as well get it over with . . .' said Ben, picking up his bag.

Ben walked over to Charlotte before his courage vanished. She was surrounded by her friends.

'Charlotte, I —' Ben began.

'What d'you want?' Charlotte asked frostily.

Not a very encouraging start!

'I . . . er . . . I want to say I'm sorry . . .' Ben began.

'For what?' asked Charlotte. 'For showing me up? For making everyone laugh at me? For using me as a joke for your friends?'

'No, it wasn't like that. I . . .'

'Is this another joke?' Charlotte's eyes narrowed.

Ben didn't get the chance to answer. Barely had he opened his mouth when he was pushed hard, sending him tumbling towards Charlotte.

'You sissy, prissy weed!'

And even before he turned around, Ben

knew who had pushed him. He spun around to face Splitter. Out of the corner of his eye, Ben saw his friends, Steven, Alex and Christopher, come to stand silently beside him. Splitter Lawson grinned at all of them. Without warning, Splitter snatched Ben's back-pack away from him.

'There's something moving in here. What've you got in here, maggot?' Splitter asked.

'Give that back.' Ben tried to grab his bag but Splitter pushed him away.

'Let's see what's in here first,' said Splitter.

'Give that back right this second or —'

'Or what?' Splitter laughed.

Ben glared at Splitter, his fists clenched, his blood roaring in his ears. Helplessly he watched as Splitter took Whizziwig out of his school-bag. Judging by the reaction of those around Ben, Splitter wasn't the only one who was surprised and curious. Ben saw that Whizziwig was careful to keep her mouth and her eyes shut and she didn't move a millimetre in Splitter's hand.

'Put that down,' Ben demanded.

'What is it?' frowned Splitter. 'Some kind of hairy football?'

Ben could stand it no longer. He jumped up suddenly, trying to snatch Whizziwig back before Splitter could stop him. It didn't work. Splitter pushed Ben so hard that Ben fell over.

'This hairy football is obviously something you want a lot . . .' Splitter grinned. 'So what will you give me to get it back?'

'Splitter, you're a pea-brained moron,' Charlotte said furiously.

'Yeah, why don't you go and play with the traffic?' said Steven, helping Ben to his feet.

Splitter frowned at the crowd in front of him. Very occasionally, one of his class would stand up to him but it was always individually – never as a group. Splitter didn't like this. Not one little bit.

'All the teachers think you're so brill and you're nothing but a bullying, stupid idiot,' Ben said furiously.

'Yeah. I wish the teachers could see you for what you really are,' Steven added.

'Yeah, so do I.'

'And me.' Others in the class began to join in.

'Hands up all those who agree,' said Steven.

Fifteen hands shot straight up into the air.

'You see! Everyone agrees with me,' Steven said coldly.

'You just wait. I'll get all of you . . .' Splitter began. 'And I'll start with this stupid football.'

And Splitter kicked Whizziwig across the classroom.

'Whizziwig!' Ben cried out desperately.

Ben ran over to where Splitter had kicked Whizziwig. She lay totally still, her eyes closed. Ben stroked her fur, trying to feel if she was still alive, but he couldn't tell. Hot, angry tears welled up in Ben's eyes. Furiously he turned back to Splitter.

'So much for your stupid, hairy football,' Splitter laughed at Ben. His smile faded as he turned to glare at all those in front of him. 'And so much for all of you. Just wait till you're all outside in the playground.'

And with that, Splitter marched out of the classroom.

Chapter Nine

Splitter Changes

There was an uncomfortable silence in the classroom when Splitter left. Slowly, everyone began to wander out. No one was looking forward to getting to the playground. Splitter would be even worse than normal now.

Ben dropped to his knees.

'Whizziwig? Whizziwig, are you all right? Speak to me,' Ben pleaded.

'Ben, what is it? What is that thing?' asked Steven from behind him.

'Whizziwig, please. Speak to me,' Ben said urgently.

'What on earth . . . You mean, that thing is *alive*?' Steven asked, his eyes bigger than saucers.

Ben took a quick look around the room. The few people left in the class were on their way out and not taking any notice of Ben or Steven.

'Her name is Whizziwig and she's from the planet Oricon,' Ben explained.

'An alien?' Steven breathed, excitedly. 'Does she have acid for blood and will she take over your body?'

'If you can't talk sense, bog off!' Ben snapped.

'Sorry!' Steven said. 'I got a bit carried away! Wait a minute, is she the reason you had all those bikes in your front garden yesterday?'

Ben nodded.

'I knew it!' said Steven.

Ben turned back to Whizziwig. Slowly her eyes fluttered open. Ben sat back on his heels and, picking up Whizziwig, hugged her tight.

'Oh, Whizziwig, I thought . . . I thought . . .' Ben couldn't say what he thought. 'Are you all right?'

'I think so,' Whizziwig whispered. She moved out of Ben's grasp and hovered upwards until she was level with Ben's face.

'What happened?' Whizziwig asked. 'All I remember is flying through the air – without my spaceship!'

'That idiot Splitter thought you were a football and kicked you,' Ben informed her, angrily.

'Splitter!' Whizziwig's eyes opened wide. 'We had better find him before anyone else does.'

'Why? What's the problem?' asked Steven.

Whizziwig turned to look at Ben's best friend. 'You! You are the one who wished that the teachers could see Splitter for what he really is. And all your friends wished the same by putting their hands up.'

'So?' Steven still didn't get it. Ben got to his feet.

'Whizziwig is an accidental wish-giver,' Ben explained. 'She grants wishes.'

'Oh? I wish I had a CD video game-player then,' Steven said immediately.

'It doesn't work like that,' Ben said impatiently.

'Quick! We have to find Splitter,' said Whizziwig.

'Why the big rush?' asked Steven.

'Did you grant Steven's wish then?' Ben asked.

'Sixteen of you made the same wish so it is bound to have worked. But I must confess that I am not one hundred per cent certain.' Whizziwig frowned. 'That moronic lout Splitter should thank his lucky stars that he kicked me when he did or he would have changed right here in the classroom. Even now I cannot be sure he *has* changed. I had to employ all my secondary energy to heal myself, leaving only my tertiary energy supply available to change him. I am not sure it was enough.'

Steven and Ben looked at each other.

'D'you know what she's talking about?' asked Steven.

'I ... er ... some of ... no!' Ben admitted.

'That does not matter. Where is Splitter now?' asked Whizziwig.

'Out in the playground, pushing everyone over I expect,' Ben predicted glumly.

'Then let us proceed.' Whizziwig bounced across the classroom and tucked herself down into Ben's bag.

Once they'd reached the playground, Ben and Steven saw a strange thing. No one was crying, there were no bruised and bleeding knees being rubbed – nothing.

'Charlotte, have you seen Splitter?' Ben asked.

'What d'you want him for?' Charlotte raised her eyebrows. 'I'd have thought you'd want to avoid him.'

'Charlotte . . .'

'Oh, all right. He ducked behind the loos about five minutes ago. Just waiting for the right moment to crash into as many people as possible I suppose,' Charlotte said with disgust. 'What a dork!'

Ben and Steven didn't wait to hear any more. They ran full pelt to the sloping alcove which housed the playground loos. These loos were avoided by everyone who didn't have a bad cold as they were so smelly!

And then they saw it. Splitter wasn't there – but a donkey was!

'Where on earth did that donkey come from?' Steven asked, amazed.

Whizziwig popped her head out of Ben's bag. 'It is not a donkey,' she said. 'It is Splitter! A jackass he is, a jackass I have changed him into and a jackass he will remain!'

Ben stared at the jackass – its long floppy

ears, its dopey expression – and burst out laughing. Steven joined in. He couldn't help it.

'That look suits him,' grinned Ben.

'It sure does,' Steven agreed. 'Now all the teachers will see Splitter for what he really is!'

Ben's grin faded. 'Hang on a minute. What're we going to do with him until tomorrow morning? We can't let anyone see him like this.'

But already someone else was wandering around the corner towards the loos.

'Hello, Steven, Ben. I thought ... I saw ...' Christopher's voice trailed off altogether. He stared and stared at the creature before him.

'Did one of you bring a donkey to school?' Christopher asked, intense admiration on his face.

'Of course not,' frowned Ben. 'And it's a jackass, not a donkey.'

'His name is Splitter,' smiled Steven.

Christopher burst out laughing. 'You'd better not let the real Splitter hear you say that,' he warned.

'Eee-aw!' the jackass brayed.

'He already knows!' Ben couldn't resist saying. And he and Steven both creased up laughing. The sound soon had more and more people coming to investigate.

'Anyone want a ride on Splitter?' Steven called out.

Ben was sorely tempted but in the end he shook his head.

'No, Steven, it wouldn't be right.'

'Eee-aw!' brayed Splitter the jackass in agreement.

'Shush, you!' said Steven, enjoying himself. He turned to Ben. 'Yes, it would be right. He deserves it.'

Ben was just about to argue when a voice boomed across the playground: 'What on earth is that donkey doing here? Who brought that donkey to school?'

And at the sound of Mr Archer approaching, everyone froze.

Chapter Ten

Call Out the RSPCA

Mr Archer glared at the jackass before turning his beady gaze on all those around him.

No one spoke.

'Where's Splitter?' asked Mr Archer. 'Whenever there's any trouble, he's usually at the back of it somewhere.'

Ben stared at the teacher – as did everyone else. Now how did he know that? Ben could've sworn that Splitter had all the teachers completely fooled.

'Stand aside,' Mr Archer ordered.

He swept through the crowd until he stood in front of Splitter the jackass.

'You will come with me,' said Mr Archer.

'Eeeee-awwww!' Splitter replied.

Mr Archer tweaked Splitter's long, floppy ears, trying to pull him forward.

'Eeeee-awwww!' Splitter brayed again.

Ben and Steven looked at each other. Ben chewed on his bottom lip. What was he going to do?

'Follow me, you stupid creature.' Mr Archer was getting annoyed now. He eyed the crowd around him. 'Ben, run to the staff-room and ask Mrs Jenkins to call out the RSPCA. Tell them there's a stray donkey in our playground.'

Ben chewed nervously on his bottom lip again. Mr Archer raised his eyebrows.

'Today, Ben! Today!' he said with sarcasm.

Ben ran off towards the staff-room as ordered. The moment he was clear of everyone else, he opened his shoulder-bag.

'Whizziwig, what're we going to do?' he asked anxiously.

'Let the RSPCA take him,' sniffed Whizziwig. 'Who else would want him?'

'His mum probably does!'

'I fail to see what all the fuss is about,' Whizziwig huffed. 'In sixteen days he will turn back into the nasty boy he is, but hopefully he will have learnt one or two manners in the meantime.'

'Sixteen days!' Ben spluttered. 'I thought Splitter was supposed to return to normal tomorrow?'

'Usually he would,' said Whizziwig. 'But in this case, Steven made his wish, and fifteen others, including you, made the same wish by putting your hands up. Therefore Splitter will remain a jackass for sixteen days. Wonderful! That leaves only one more item on my ship still to fix.'

'Whizziwig, what's going to happen when he doesn't get home tonight? And if the RSPCA take him, he'll end up on a farm or in a zoo or something. You've got to change him back,' said Ben.

'Impossible,' said Whizziwig. 'I think I will shut down for an hour or so. All the excitement has quite depleted my energy reserves.'

And Whizziwig ducked back down into Ben's bag before he could say another word.

'Whizziwig? Whizziwig, you can't go to sleep now,' Ben protested.

But the silence echoing from his bag showed that she already had!

When Ben told Mrs Jenkins about a jack-ass being in the playground, she didn't believe him until she'd looked out of the staff-room window and checked for herself. And even when she phoned the RSPCA she still kept shaking her head and staring out of the window as if she couldn't believe her own eyes!

After the morning break, it was impossible to do any work. Everyone was too busy staring out of the classroom windows at the solitary figure in the playground. Splitter the jackass stood all alone. And even though Ben thought Splitter was a bullying dork, he still felt kind of sorry for him.

Ben's conscience poked and prodded and gnawed away at him until at last he felt he had to say something. Slowly he put his hand up.

'Yes, Ben? What is it?' asked Mr Archer.

'Sir, I know where the jackass came from,' Ben said reluctantly.

'Oh?'

'It's ... it's Splitter. He's been changed into a jackass so all the teachers can see what he's really like.'

Mr Archer scowled as the rest of the class howled with laughter.

'Very funny, Ben. Up here! Now!'

'But, sir . . .' Ben protested.

'NOW!'

And once again Ben found himself swapping places with Thea and sitting in front of the teacher's desk.

'I don't know what's got into you over the last couple of days, Ben Sinclair,' Mr Archer said testily. 'But you can just get it out again! I won't stand for such behaviour.'

'No, sir,' Ben said, miserably.

What else can go wrong? Ben thought with a silent sigh.

He was going to find out!

Chapter Eleven

Taking a Risk

At lunch-time, Mr Archer made Ben sit outside the staff-room for being cheeky.

'Whizziwig, wake up!' Ben shook his bag gently. '*Please* wake up!'

'What *is* the matter?' Whizziwig asked crossly. 'Granting sixteen wishes at once is very tiring. You should try it some time.'

'Whizziwig –' Ben got no further, for just at that moment the staff-room door opened and Mrs Jenkins strode out. Whizziwig only just managed to duck down into Ben's bag without being seen.

'Mrs Jenkins, can I ask you something?' Ben said.

'Oh, er . . . yes, Ben?'

'What will happen to Splitt – I mean,

the jackass in the playground when the
RSPCA take him?' asked Ben.

'Well, the RSPCA will look after him for a
short while, but if they can't find somewhere
permanent for the donkey to stay, I guess . . .
I guess they'll have to put him down,' said
Mrs Jenkins.

'Put him down?' Ben was shocked.

'It is the kindest thing they can do in the

circumstances.' Mrs Jenkins placed an understanding hand on Ben's shoulder.

'How long will they wait before they do that?' Ben could hardly get the words out.

'A couple of weeks?' Mrs Jenkins shrugged her shoulders. 'I've got to go, Ben. Talk to Mr Archer if you have any more questions.'

And Mrs Jenkins marched off.

Ben swallowed hard and had to keep swallowing to stop himself from being sick. They were going to put Splitter to sleep – for ever.

'Whizziwig, you *must* do something ...' Ben whispered urgently once he was sure the coast was clear. Ben struggled to remember something that Whizziwig had said to him when they'd first met.

'Whizziwig, didn't you say something about your wishes lasting ninety thousand odd yenvings except in special circumstances?' Ben remembered.

'That's true, but –' Whizziwig began.

'This is a special circumstance,' Ben interrupted. 'So you must change him back.'

'I can only revoke one of my wishes in extremely special and hazardous circumstances,' Whizziwig said. 'And you are not asking me to revoke one of my wishes, but sixteen of them.'

'We have no choice,' Ben pleaded. 'We must change Splitter back.'

'I might be able to do it but I do not know if I will be able to reactivate afterwards.'

'What does that mean?' Ben asked. He wasn't sure, but whatever it was, it didn't sound too good.

'It means,' said Whizziwig gently, 'that if I do reverse all those wishes at once, it will drain my energy so much that I'll shut down immediately . . . but I don't know if I'll have enough energy to wake up again.'

Ben stared at Whizziwig, horrified.

'If this happened on my home planet of Oricon, I would be taken to the reactivation centre and would be fully functional again within forty-four thousand yenvings, but as it is . . .' Whizziwig didn't finish her sentence. She didn't have to.

'What are we going to do?' Ben asked, stricken.

Whizziwig smiled. 'As you said, we cannot let Splitter be put down. It is a risk I shall have to take. But I am doing it for you, not for Splitter.'

Ben shook his head miserably. Even as a jackass, Splitter was still causing all kinds of trouble. For a second Ben was tempted to tell Whizziwig to forget about Splitter and save herself, but he knew he couldn't do that. If anything happened to Splitter, Ben would never forgive himself. But what about Whizziwig?

'I had better get started,' sighed Whizziwig. 'This is going to take some time.'

And she ducked down into Ben's back-pack.

Ben spent a very miserable lunch-time, frequently glancing down at his watch and wondering if he was letting Whizziwig do the right thing. Deep down, he knew he was but that didn't make things any easier.

Occasionally, Ben whispered to his bag, 'Whizziwig, are you OK?'

And she replied, 'I am working!'

But as time went on, her voice began to fade and her words grew softer and softer.

'Ben, the RSPCA have arrived. They're going to take Splitter away.' Steven hopped up and down in front of Ben. 'We've got to do something.'

'Whizziwig is working on it,' Ben said. He had to swallow hard before he could say anything else. 'Where're the RSPCA now?'

'In the playground with Splitter,' Steven replied, still hopping about anxiously.

Ben and Steven ran into the nearest classroom which overlooked the playground. There, three teachers – including Mr Archer – and three RSPCA officials were trying to load Splitter the jackass into a small horsebox. But Splitter wasn't having any! He kicked and brayed and tossed his head and

made it impossible for anyone to get near him.

'Hold him!'

'Watch out!'

'Mind his back legs!'

Even from where Ben was standing he could hear the grown-ups calling out to each other.

Splitter the jackass spun around and kicked out like a bucking bronco in a Wild West film, then he made a break for it towards the playground toilets.

'Stop! Come back!' The RSPCA and the teachers gave chase.

Ben closed his eyes, but opened them immediately. It was even more nerve-racking *not* seeing what was going on!

'Splitter's disappeared round the corner,' Steven told him breathlessly. 'He must be hiding in one of the loos.'

The RSPCA people and the teachers were only a few seconds behind Splitter, but the moment they turned into the alcove, they froze.

What's going on now? Ben thought desperately.

Mr Archer marched further around the corner and out of sight whilst the other grown-ups stayed where they were, staring into the alcove. Within moments Mr Archer appeared, his hand grasped tightly around Splitter's arm. Splitter was a boy again, back to his normal self. But judging from the nuclear look on Mr Archer's face, Splitter was in a great deal of trouble.

'I don't know how you did it and I don't care,' said Mr Archer as he marched across the playground with Splitter in tow. 'But you *don't* bring a donkey to school and you *don't* waste my time or any other teacher's time with your foolishness and you *don't* play stupid tricks with your pets.'

'But, Mr Archer –' Splitter began. He got no further.

'I'm going to call up your parents and they can pay for the RSPCA people being called out on a wild-goose chase!' Mr Archer continued.

Ben saw an RSPCA official come out of the playground alcove, take off his cap and scratch his head, very puzzled indeed.

'Thank goodness for that.' Steven turned

his back on the window and slumped against it.

'Whizziwig, are you all right?' Ben opened up his shoulder-bag.

There lay Whizziwig, her eyes closed. She was less than half her normal size, like a balloon with most of its air let out, and her golden fur was now a dingy, muddy colour.

Chapter Twelve

Thirty Voices, One Wish

'What happened?' Steven asked, aghast. 'Whizziwig's exhausted. She had to use all her primary, secondary and tertiary energy to change Splitter back into a boy.' Ben's eyes were stinging. 'And now she might never wake up.'

'But she must,' Steven said, shocked. 'Do something.'

'Like what?' Ben snapped. 'Don't you think I would if I could?'

'Wish for her to be well again,' Steven said.

'I'm not sure that would do it,' Ben said slowly.

'We've got to do something . . .' Steven said.

A tiny seed of an idea dropped into Ben's head.

'Steven, you and me have to get everyone in our class together during the afternoon break. And in the next lesson we've got to write out thirty wishes,' Ben said. 'I've thought of something that just might work.'

And Ben told Steven his plan.

The afternoon clock ticked so slowly that Ben was sure it was doing it on purpose. Mr Archer wittered on about fractions, suspiciously glancing around the room from time to time because everyone was so quiet.

At last the buzzer sounded.

'OK, everyone, we'll carry on with . . .' Mr Archer didn't bother to finish his sentence. He was completely alone. He'd never seen his class beetle out of the classroom so quickly to get to the playground!

'If only they showed the same eagerness for fractions,' the teacher muttered to himself.

Ben was one of the last ones in his class to make it to the playground alcove. Steven stood guard to make sure that none of the teachers were near by.

'Have you really got an alien, Ben?'

'Let me see . . .'

'Show me . . .'

'Shush!' Ben quietened down the crowd around him. Slowly he opened up his bag. Whizziwig was now the size of a tennis ball and still shrinking.

'Ooooh!'

'Wow!'

'Wait until I tell my sister tonight!' said Charlotte.

'Not much of an alien . . .' said Paul,
unimpressed.

'Shut up, Paul. Are you going to help us
or not?' asked Steven crossly.

'Yeah, of course,' Paul replied.

'Her name is Whizziwig and she needs
your help,' Ben said. 'She used up all her
energy changing Splitter the jackass back
into Splitter the boy and now we've got to
help her get her energy back.'

'How do we do that?' asked Charlotte.

Very carefully, Ben picked up Whizziwig and placed her gently on his bag in the middle of the crowd. Then he and Steven got out lots of bits of paper from their pockets and started handing them out.

'I'll count to three,' said Ben. 'And then we've all got to say what's written on the paper *altogether, at the same time.* It's really important that we all speak at the same time. That way all thirty of us will make just one wish and it'll be stronger.'

'Are you sure?' asked Christopher.

'No,' Ben admitted. 'But we've got to do something and Whizziwig did say that she got her energy from wishes.'

'Only this time we're going to make a wish for her,' Steven added.

'Stand back, everyone, and join hands,' said Ben.

Soon everyone was standing in a circle, their hands joined.

'One . . . two . . . three . . .' Ben counted.

And everyone said, 'We wish Whizziwig would get well again!'

Ben looked down at Whizziwig anxiously. Nothing was happening.

'Everyone say it again,' Ben called out.

'We wish Whizziwig would get well again! We wish Whizziwig would get well again!'

It happened so slowly that at first Ben wasn't sure if he was seeing things.

'Something's going on . . .' Steven whispered from beside him.

And sure enough Whizziwig began to get BIGGER and BIGGER and BIGGER.

'Keep wishing!' Ben called out excitedly.

'We wish Whizziwig would get well again!'

When Whizziwig was the size of a football she started to hover very gently off the ground. Her fur began to glow strangely. Whizziwig continued to float upwards until she was about level with everyone's head. Then she opened her eyes. A few of the boys took a hasty step backwards. A couple of the girls gasped. Ben dashed forward.

'Whizziwig! Are you OK?'

Whizziwig turned around in mid-air to face Ben. The others in Ben's class moved slowly forward.

'Wow! She's real!'

'A real live alien!'

'She doesn't look anything like in the films . . .'

'Whizziwig, are you . . .' But Ben got no further.

Before everyone's eyes, Whizziwig smiled and with a sudden POP! she vanished like a washing-up bubble.

Chapter Thirteen

Whizziwig Says Goodbye

Ben never knew how he got through the rest of the day. He had a horrible pain in his chest that wouldn't go away, no matter what he did. Steven and Christopher did their best to cheer him up but it was no good. Ben wanted to run away and hide from everyone. He had failed . . .

When at last it was time to go home, Ben couldn't even speak. He felt that if he moved his mouth, even a little bit, his whole face would crumble and fall apart.

'Shall I walk home with you?' asked Steven.

Ben shook his head. He didn't want any company – ever again. Ben swung his bag over his shoulder. Without Whizziwig it felt strangely light and empty. He walked up to the school exit, his head bent. He was aware that others in his class were talking about him.

'Ben, she was a very pretty alien – even if she didn't last very long,' Charlotte said.

Ben couldn't answer. He wanted Whizzi-wig back. He wanted to say he was sorry for causing all her energy to drain away and he wanted to ask her about her home planet and he wanted . . . he wanted more time. Which was the one thing he didn't have. Whizziwig was gone.

Ben carried on walking.

It took longer than usual for Ben to reach his house, as he didn't exactly race home. The moment he stepped foot over the front door, Tarzan came bounding up to him.

'Down, Tarzan. Down!' Ben ordered.

Tarzan lay down immediately. Ben stroked the fur between the dog's ears.

'Hi, Ben,' Mum shouted from the living-room. 'How are you?'

'OK . . .' Ben called back, before running upstairs. He didn't even want to talk to his mum. Ben pushed open his bedroom door and – WOW!

The whole room was filled with a dazzling golden light that lit up every nook and cranny and corner. And there, hovering in the middle of the room, was the Oricon.

'Whizziwig!' Ben exclaimed.

In about two seconds flat, Ben was in the middle of the room and hugging Whizziwig as hard as he could.

'I had one wish left to grant when you and your friends wished that I would get well again.' Whizziwig smiled. 'It was very kind of you. All of you wishing for the same thing made it happen.'

'Oh, Whizziwig, am I glad to see you. I thought . . . I thought . . .' Ben didn't want to think about what he'd thought.

'I am fine. My ship is outside your window, fully repaired. Come and see,' said Whizziwig.

Ben rushed to the window and peered out. There, floating about a metre away from his windowsill was a large, spherical, almost transparent ship. It glowed a radiant gold and silver, almost dazzling Ben. Ben could see all kinds of controls and levers and buttons and gadgets all over the ship.

'It's the most beautiful spaceship I've ever seen,' Ben breathed.

In the centre of the ship was what looked like a round fruit-bowl.

'What's that bowl thing?' Ben asked, pointing.

'Bowl? That is my chair. I must have somewhere to sit,' Whizziwig laughed.

'You're . . . you're not really going yet, are you?' Ben asked.

'I have to. I am already late as it is. You would not want my aunt to worry, would you – any more than you wanted Splitter's mum to worry about him,' Whizziwig said.

'I guess not,' Ben said slowly.

'Anyway, the good news is, I do not think Splitter will be such a pest in future.' Whizziwig winked. 'I have a feeling he is going to remember how it felt to be a jackass for a long, long time.'

Ben remembered how his neighbour Mrs Leonard kept slapping her hand over her mouth when she talked to him as the fire brigade got rid of the bicycles in his garden. She wasn't about to forget how it felt to have her tongue hinged in the middle either.

'Whizziwig, take me with you. I'd love to see Oricon,' said Ben.

'Nope, I cannot. Besides, where would you sit? But maybe next time I will travel in a bigger ship and we will go and visit my aunt together.'

'Next time? There'll be a next time? D'you promise?' Ben said eagerly.

Whizziwig thought hard for a moment. 'Yup, I promise,' she said at last. 'Now I really must be going.'

'Couldn't you go tomorrow or the next day?' Ben asked.

Whizziwig rocked from side to side. 'Ben, I will be back. Did I not just promise?'

Ben nodded.

'I'm really glad you're better now,' he said.

'Thanks to you and your friends. Thank them all for me the next time you see them.' And with that, Whizziwig bounced out of Ben's bedroom and into her spaceship.

'Take care, Ben,' said Whizziwig.

'Wait. . .' Ben began.

But already Whizziwig's spaceship was rising into the air.

'Goodbye, Ben, my first friend on this planet,' Whizziwig called out.

And as Ben watched, the spaceship rose higher and higher into the sky. He was all mixed up. Part of him was so glad that Whizziwig was indeed all right, but another part of him didn't want to see her go. There was so much he still wanted to ask her, so much he still wanted to find out.

'Ben, dear, could you come downstairs for a moment?' Ben's mum called out.

Ben went downstairs, still feeling strangely mixed up.

Ben's mum and dad were standing in the living-room, hugging each other.

'We've got some news for you,' smiled Dad.

'Some good news,' Mum added.

'Oh! You needn't get me a mountain bike after all,' Ben shrugged. 'I guess I can make do with my old bike for a bit longer.'

'Our news is a bit more exciting than a

mouldy mountain bike, Ben,' Dad laughed. 'Your mum's pregnant. In a few months you're going to have a baby brother or sister.'

Ben's mouth fell open. 'I am?' he squeaked.

'You are,' Mum laughed.

Ben ran through the house and flung open the front door.

'Whizziwig! I'm going to have a baby brother or sister!' Ben shouted as loudly as he could.

Ben's mum and dad came out of the living-room to stand behind him.

'Who's Whizziwig?' asked his mum.

'I wished for a brother or sister and now I'm going to get one,' Ben beamed. 'Whizziwig's the one who made it possible.'

His mum and dad looked at each other.

'Ben, you're a strange child,' his mum smiled.

'Whizziwig, thank you!' Ben called out again. 'Come back soon!'

And high, high above him, Ben was sure he saw a silver and golden light twinkle at him with a brightness that dazzled.